if

Rudyard Kipling
& Giovanni Manna

Creative Editions

Introduction

What parent does not wish the best for a child? And what child has not experienced—if only for a moment—the desire to live up to parental expectations? Imagine how such feelings are compounded when children grow up in the shadow of a sibling's death. In 1899, Rudyard and Carrie Kipling lost their eldest daughter, then six, to a sudden illness. Their family circle forever changed, the Kiplings became even more tightly knit, and the two younger children were perhaps more cherished than ever before. Elsie and John grew up with a father who doted on them, who read to them, who answered ceaseless questions, who indulged their imaginations. Yet he also expected great things of them.

Especially great were Kipling's aspirations for his only son, to whom he directed his words with the poem "If—," written sometime in 1909 before its original publication in 1910 as part of the short story collection *Rewards and Fairies*. Kipling's long fascination with military life began in books, and he wanted his son to pursue the naval career he never could. Unfortunately for John (and his father), he inherited Kipling's poor eyesight. That seemed to rule out becoming a sailor or soldier. A Kipling biographer described young John as "a straightforward, popular, and good-natured boy, with quick wit, a great sense of fun and much charm, but with no marked talents." Still, John was sent to a boarding school for military training at the age of 14, and his devoted dad visited him as often as he could.

In August 1914, England declared war on Germany, and 17-year-old John wanted nothing more than to enlist as a private soldier. His famous father called in a favor to a friend in charge of a regiment known as the Irish Guards, and by mid-September, John was reporting for duty. The boy "with no marked talents" showed courage beyond his years the following September, during the Battle of Loos. There he led his battalion across dangerous ground, never to return.

Today, "If—" remains one of the most popular poems in its native England and around the world, and it is often quoted for its inspirational quality. Not only is it an expression of advice to children, but it is also a poem that can speak to anyone at any stage in life—*if* we care to listen.

if

you can keep your head when all about you
Are losing theirs and blaming it on you,

if

you can trust yourself when all men doubt you,
But make allowance for their doubting too:

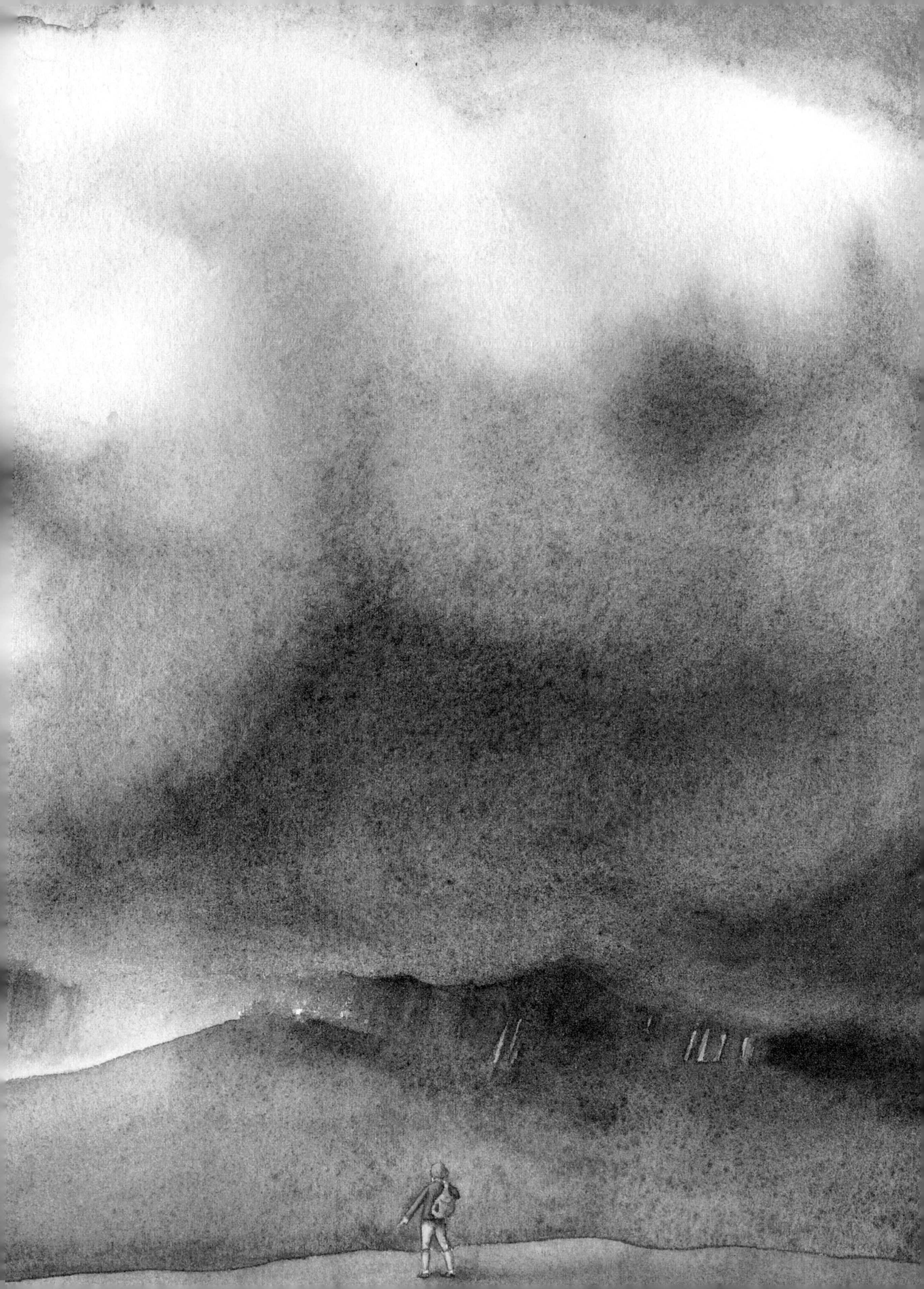

if you can wait and not be tired by waiting,

Or being lied about, don't deal in lies,

Or being hated, don't give way to hating,

And yet don't look too good, nor talk too wise:

if
you can dream—and not make dreams your master;

if you can think—and not make thoughts your aim;

If you can meet with Triumph and Disaster

And treat those two impostors just the same;

if you can bear to hear the truth you've spoken
Twisted by knaves to make a trap for fools,

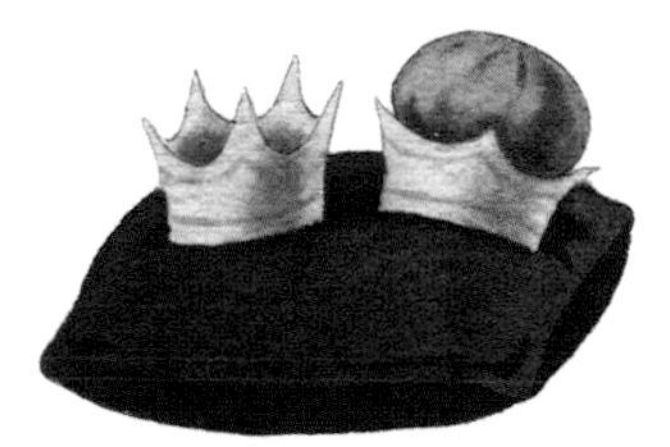

OR watch the things you gave your life to, broken,

And stoop and build 'em up with worn-out tools:

if

you can make one heap of all your winnings
And risk it on one turn of pitch-and-toss,
And lose, and start again at your beginnings
And never breathe a word about your loss;

if you can force your heart and nerve and sinew
To serve your turn long after they are gone,
And so hold on when there is nothing in you
Except the Will which says to them: "Hold on!"

OR
watch the things you gave your life to, broken,

And stoop and build 'em up with worn-out tools:

if you can make one heap of all your winnings
And risk it on one turn of pitch-and-toss,
And lose, and start again at your beginnings
And never breathe a word about your loss;

if

you can force your heart and nerve and sinew
    To serve your turn long after they are gone,
And so hold on when there is nothing in you
    Except the Will which says to them: "Hold on!"

if you can talk with crowds and keep your virtue,

Or walk with Kings—nor lose the common touch,

if

neither foes nor loving friends can hurt you,

If all men count with you, but none too much;

if

you can fill the unforgiving minute

With sixty seconds' worth of distance run,

yours

is the Earth and everything that's in it,

And—which is more—you'll be a Man, my son!

if

If you can keep your head when all about you
Are losing theirs and blaming it on you,
If you can trust yourself when all men doubt you,
But make allowance for their doubting too:
If you can wait and not be tired by waiting,
Or being lied about, don't deal in lies,
Or being hated, don't give way to hating,
And yet don't look too good, nor talk too wise:

If you can dream—and not make dreams your master;
If you can think—and not make thoughts your aim;
If you can meet with Triumph and Disaster
And treat those two impostors just the same;
If you can bear to hear the truth you've spoken
Twisted by knaves to make a trap for fools,
Or watch the things you gave your life to, broken,
And stoop and build 'em up with worn-out tools:

If you can make one heap of all your winnings
And risk it on one turn of pitch-and-toss,
And lose, and start again at your beginnings
And never breathe a word about your loss;
If you can force your heart and nerve and sinew
To serve your turn long after they are gone,
And so hold on when there is nothing in you
Except the Will which says to them: "Hold on!"

If you can talk with crowds and keep your virtue,
Or walk with Kings—nor lose the common touch,
If neither foes nor loving friends can hurt you,
If all men count with you, but none too much;
If you can fill the unforgiving minute
With sixty seconds' worth of distance run,
Yours is the Earth and everything that's in it,
And—which is more—you'll be a Man, my son!

To my son and daughters, may the Earth and everything that's in it be yours.
Tom Peterson, publisher

Published in 2014 by Creative Editions
P.O. Box 227, Mankato, MN 56002 USA
Creative Editions is an imprint of The Creative Company
www.thecreativecompany.us
Designed by Rita Marshall

Printed in China
Library of Congress Cataloging-in-Publication Data
Kipling, Rudyard, 1865–1936, author.
If— / by Rudyard Kipling; illustrated by Giovanni Manna.
Summary: The famously inspirational poem written by Rudyard Kipling,
which first appeared in a 1910 collection of short stories and poems,
is here accompanied by illustrations.
ISBN 978-1-56846-259-2
1. Fathers and sons—Poetry. I. Manna, Giovanni, 1966– illustrator. II. Title.
PR4854.I4 2014 821'.8—dc23 2013028606

First Edition
2 4 6 8 9 7 5 3 1

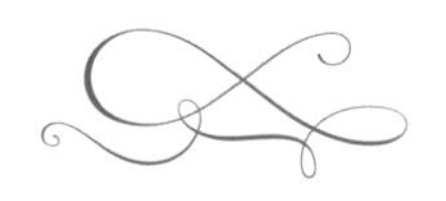